KT-513-570

SAM SILVER: UNDERCOVER PIRATE

THE
DOUBLE-CROSS

Collect all the Sam Silver: Undercover Pirate *books*

THE DOUBLE-CROSS

Jan Burchett and Sara Vogler

Illustrated by Leo Hartas

Orion
Children's Books

First published in Great Britain in 2013
by Orion Children's Books
a division of the Orion Publishing Group Ltd
Orion House
5 Upper St Martin's Lane
London WC2H 9EA
An Hachette UK company

3 5 7 9 10 8 6 4 2

Text copyright © Jan Burchett and Sara Vogler 2013
Map and interior illustrations copyright © Leo Hartas 2013

The right of Jan Burchett and Sara Vogler to be identified
as the authors of this work, and the right of Leo Hartas to be
identified as the illustrator of this work have been asserted.

All rights reserved. No part of this publication may be reproduced,
stored in a retrieval system, or transmitted, in any form or by any means,
electronic, mechanical, photocopying, recording or otherwise,
without the prior permission of Orion Children's Books.

The Orion Publishing Group's policy is to use papers that are
natural, renewable and recyclable products and made from wood grown
in sustainable forests. The logging and manufacturing processes are expected
to conform to the environmental regulations of the country of origin.

A catalogue record for this book is available from the British Library.

ISBN 978 1 4440 0589 9

Printed in Great Britain by Clays Ltd, St Ives plc

For Phill Seiler,
Pyjama Angel Supreme.

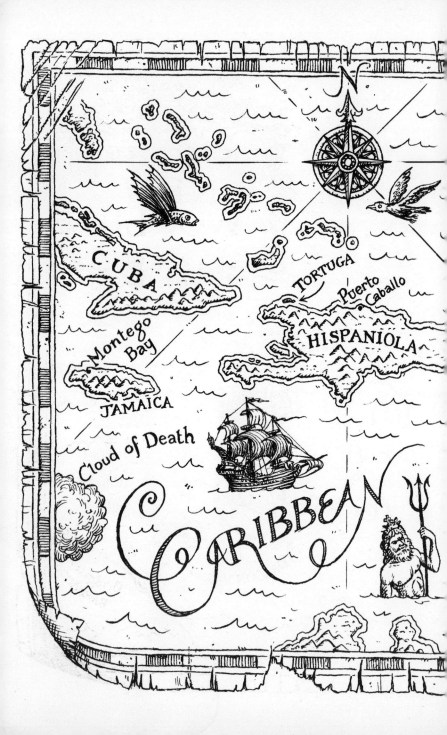

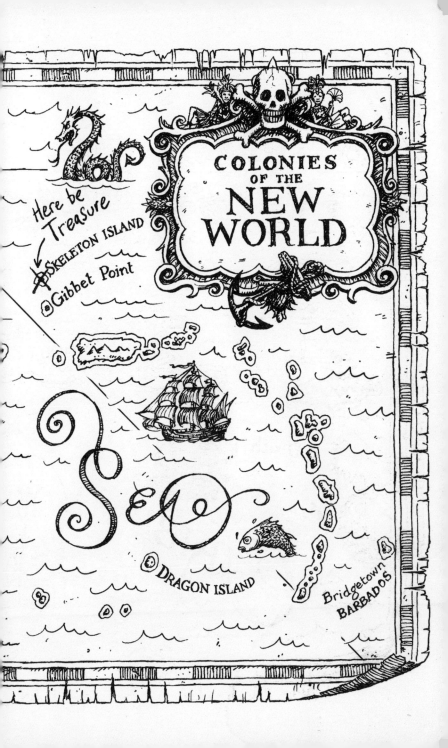

COLONIES
OF THE
NEW
WORLD

Here be
Treasure

SKELETON ISLAND

Gibbet Point

Sea

DRAGON ISLAND

Bridgetown
BARBADOS

The SEA WOLF

Captain's Cabin
Hammocks
Gun Deck
Galley
Ship's Stores

CHAPTER ONE

Sam Silver sat in his bedroom chewing
his pencil. He was supposed to
be doing a school project. Everyone in
the class had to design a shield to show
something interesting about their family.
And it had to be ready tomorrow.

Sam was stuck. His mum and dad ran
The Jolly Cod, the only fish and chip shop
in Backwater Bay, and they all lived in the

flat above. So Sam had drawn a bit of
battered haddock and a bag of chips on
his coat of arms, but he didn't think his
teacher would be very impressed.

He gazed round his room, desperately
trying to dream up something really
amazing about his family. His eyes fell upon
the old bottle he'd discovered on the beach.
Inside he'd found a dirty old gold coin sent
to him by a pirate ancestor called Joseph
Silver. When he'd tried to clean it, the
doubloon had whisked him back in time to
the *Sea Wolf,* a pirate ship in the Caribbean.

He'd joined Captain Blade's crew and now, whenever he rubbed the coin, he zoomed back to 1706 ready for another adventure.

Sam leapt to his feet. Of course! He knew exactly what he was going to draw on his shield – the *Sea Wolf*.

Then he had an even better idea. He'd pop off to see his pirate friends right now. After all, he wanted to get his drawing of the ship perfect on his shield – and he couldn't possibly do that without going back and seeing her again. And no one would know he'd gone. Sam could keep his time travels a secret because no time ever passed in the present while he was being a bold buccaneer.

Sam rifled through the untidy pile of clothes on his bedroom floor. At the bottom of the heap were the tatty old jeans and T-shirt that he always wore for his pirate adventures. He pulled them on, tied his trainer laces and tipped the coin out of its bottle. It gleamed invitingly in his hand. He couldn't wait. Fizzing with excitement, like a bottle of lemonade that had been given a good shake, Sam spat on the coin and rubbed it on his sleeve. His project, his pile of clothes and his bedroom furniture all whirled past in a blur. He clamped his fingers round the doubloon and shut his eyes, feeling as if he was being sucked into a giant vacuum cleaner.

He landed with a bump on a wooden floor and opened his eyes. He was back in the storeroom of the *Sea Wolf*. Up on deck all his friends would be hard at work. He couldn't wait to see them. As usual, Sam's friend Charlie had put his pirate clothes on a barrel ready for him. Charlie, who'd joined the crew on the run from her evil stepfather, was the only one who knew he was a time traveller. The others believed that he just slipped off home now and again to see his mother. And as all pirates loved their mums, this was all right by them.

Sam quickly pulled on his jerkin, tied his kerchief round his neck and stuck his spyglass in his belt. He flung open the storeroom door ready to leap up the steps to the main deck when something stopped him in his tracks. The only sound that reached him was the lapping of the waves against the hull. Why couldn't he hear the sails being hauled or shipmates shouting to each other and singing sea shanties? Something was wrong.

His heart in his mouth, Sam crept slowly up the staircase. He heard a deep laugh from the deck. But it wasn't one of the crew. It was an evil laugh that chilled Sam to the bone. He edged up a little until his eyes were level with the deck.

He gulped in horror. Captain Blade and the crew had been herded together against the port rail, and a bunch of cut-throat pirates were threatening them with cutlasses. Sam's friend Fernando was looking pale under his wild, curly hair, and Charlie was clinging to his arm for support. Ben Hudson, the quartermaster, was crouched on the deck, his head in his hands, and even big cheerful Ned Wainwright looked as if he was going to be sick.

Lording it over them from the rail of the deck above was a tall figure. Sam recognised that hard, cruel face with the eye patch and the grizzled beard. It was Blackheart, the nastiest pirate in the Caribbean. Sam felt as if someone had stabbed a knife into his heart. Captain Blade's mortal enemy had captured the *Sea Wolf* and taken the whole crew prisoner.

Sam knew his crew were the bravest pirates ever to sail the Seven Seas, yet here they were, pale as ghosts, bent double and cowering in fright. And bold Captain Blade, who was frightened of no man, was almost on his knees. Was he pleading with Blackheart?

Sam rubbed his eyes and looked again at the crew. Now he could see that they were all holding their stomachs. He could hear groaning. They weren't frightened – they were in pain! What had Blackheart done to them?

Sam tiptoed back down the steps. He had to make a plan to rescue his crew. But at that moment something sharp seized his shoulder in a vice-like grip.

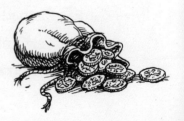

CHAPTER TWO

Sam slowly turned to face his captor and found himself staring into the two beady eyes of the ship's parrot. Crow peered at him with his head on one side and opened his beak ready to start chattering.

"Shh!" warned Sam. "You must keep quiet. It's very important."

He knew that one squawk from his

green feathered friend would bring Blackheart's men running. But Crow wasn't taking any notice.

"Aye aye!" he chirped cheerily.

"Who's there?" came a rough cry, and Sam heard footsteps thumping over the deck above. He quickly slipped back into the storeroom and hid under some sacking.

"Nothing here, Captain," came the voice again and the footsteps faded.

Sam knew he had to be quick if he was going to rescue his crew – Blackheart wasn't making a social call.

But how could he do it? There was no way he was going to pop up from the storeroom again – he'd probably get his head blown off and that wouldn't help his friends. Then he had a brilliant idea. If he made his way to one of the portholes he could climb the outside of the ship's hull and sneak up on Blackheart from behind. He'd take the evil pirate captain prisoner and make him set the *Sea Wolf* crew free.

He lifted Crow onto a barrel. "Stay here," he hissed.

He tiptoed swiftly across the gun deck, trying not to make a sound on the wooden boards. Through the portholes he could see Blackheart's ship, the *Grinning Skull*, alongside. Boarding ropes ran between them, holding the two vessels together. He passed the rows of cannon, and found the cutlass chest thrown open. It was empty. Blackheart's villains must be stealing everything they could. Then he noticed a glint of metal between the cannon. It was a cutlass. The thieves had dropped one! Well, Sam Silver, undercover pirate, wasn't going to face

Blackheart without a weapon. He thrust it into his belt.

But then he had a thought. There might not be any weapons left but the villains hadn't taken the cannonballs or powder yet. When he'd freed the crew and they were sailing away, they'd need something to defend themselves with in case Blackheart came after them. He remembered that one of the floorboards by the end cannon was loose. He hoped that they hadn't mended it since his last visit. He gave it a pull and, to his relief, it moved aside to reveal a deep gap between the decks. He ran over to the big crate strapped to the floor, where he knew some cannonballs and powder were kept ready for action. He staggered backwards and forwards to the hiding place, packing in a powder keg and as many of the heavy balls as he could. His foot caught on something. As he peered down in the gloom he realised it was the ship's flag. The enemy must have torn it down when they captured the ship. He bundled it into the hiding place. He couldn't bear the thought of Blackheart destroying this symbol of the noble *Sea Wolf*.

Now to rescue the crew. He scampered to one of the gun ports at the stern of the ship. He'd climb up to the poop deck in seconds, and before Blackheart knew what was happening the evil pirate would feel the prick of a cutlass in his back. Sam knew it was dangerous but he wasn't a Silver for nothing.

He heard footsteps. He ducked down behind a cannon just as one of Blackheart's men appeared at the other end of the deck. As the man began to hunt round, Sam could see he was a mean-looking buccaneer with small eyes, a down-turned mouth and a hooked nose.

Carefully Sam drew his weapon. *Come*

any closer, Hooknose, he thought to himself, *and you'll have a fight on your hands!*

He caught a flash of green feathers at the storeroom door and heard a loud squawk. "You scurvy knave!"

The man spun round and headed off towards the sound.

"Thanks, Crow," muttered Sam. His parrot was the perfect decoy. As silently as he could, Sam heaved himself up onto the edge of the gun port.

"Oh, no, you don't," said a gruff voice. Sam turned to find Hooknose running across the gun deck towards him, his sword ready to strike Sam down. "I had a feeling in me bones there was someone skulking down here."

Sam leaped at him, swiping the air with his cutlass. He wasn't going to let himself be taken. The lives of the crew depended on him being free.

Hooknose gave a cruel laugh.

"Think you can beat me, you young
whippersnapper?" The two blades clanged
together. Sam dodged the next blow
and bounded lightly out of reach. A
look of fury came over the attacker's
face as he realised that Sam was fast on
his feet.

"I'm going to get you, boy," he growled.
"The others said the crew were all
captured so I'm going to look really

good when I haul you up in front of
Captain Blackheart. He's sure to give
me a handsome reward. More if you're
dead!"

He lunged viciously. Sam blocked the
blow, backed off to avoid the razor-sharp
edge and found himself trapped against a
cannon. He'd have to trick his way out and
he knew just how to do it. It had worked
at school, when the bully in the year above
had cornered him in the stock cupboard.
He glanced over the man's shoulder and
grinned as if he could see a friend coming
to rescue him. Hooknose swung round to
look, and as he did so Sam gave him a
hard shove, knocking the cutlass from his
hand and sending him sprawling. It wasn't
quite so spectacular as the time at school
– the bully had got covered in white paint
and went round all day looking like a
ghost – but it still worked.

Sam cast a glance at the portholes.

Maybe he could slip through one of them before his enemy got to his feet. Too late. Hooknose was already reaching for his sword.

MEROW! A wild ball of mangy fur flew through the air, landing on the man's back. Sinbad, the ship's cat, had arrived in the nick of time. Hooknose stumbled forwards, the cat clinging grimly to his jerkin. He banged his head on a cannon and slumped to the deck.

"He's out cold!" exclaimed Sam, nudging his assailant with the toe of his trainer, just to make sure. "Thanks for coming to my rescue, Sinbad!"

The cat gave him a baleful look. Sinbad was fiercely loyal to the *Sea Wolf* crew but only Charlie was allowed to get within a paw's reach of him.

Sam climbed out of the gun port and eased himself up the side of the ship until he had his hands on the poop deck rail. He checked out the scene. The swaggering pirate captain had his back to him, heaping insults down on the *Sea Wolf* crew. No one on the deck below could see Sam as he crept up behind Blackheart.

"Captain!" It was Hooknose, staggering groggily across the deck from the storeroom stairs. "Look out!"

Blackheart whipped round. In an instant his sword was in his hand. Sam ducked the swishing blade, thinking quickly. He knew he couldn't match the fearsome pirate's strength and skill, but if he could get above him, he'd have an advantage.

He put his cutlass between his teeth and seized the rigging. As Blackheart lunged again, Sam swung himself out of reach. With a curse, the angry pirate set off after him.

"Up aloft, me hearty!" Crow came
swooping straight at Blackheart's head,
knocking his hat into his eyes. This was
Sam's chance. While his enemy clung to
the rigging, blinded by his hat, he'd
scramble up to the crow's nest and slice
through the rigging. Blackheart wouldn't
be able to follow him if he was plunging
to the deck!

"Avast ye!" came Blackheart's
bloodcurdling cry.

Sam looked down and froze in terror. A gleaming flintlock pistol was aimed right at Sam's chest. The pirate's finger tensed on the trigger.

"You can make your way to the deck like a good boy and join your crew," he snarled, "or I can blow you to kingdom come." He grinned horribly. "Your choice."

CHAPTER THREE

Blackheart's smile sent showers of ice down Sam's spine. Two grim-faced buccaneers plucked him from the rigging, snatched his cutlass and spyglass and threw him sprawling on the deck with the rest of his crew.

"Be there more of your scurvy friends skulking below?" sneered Blackheart. "I'd hate for any of 'em to miss walking the plank. I did think of running you all through, quick and easy, but then I had a better idea." He turned his head to gaze at a distant island. It was bleak and grey and desolate. "I saw that enchanting little rock yonder and I thought, why should I dirty my nice steel on you bilge rats when I could offer you a new home instead?"

His ugly band of pirates gave evil sniggers.

"If you survive the swim, I'll wager you'll not survive many days in that cursed place," Blackheart went on, a nasty gleam in his eyes. "You'll go mad and kill each other, if you don't starve to death first, and I'll be shot of me mortal enemy at last."

Sam watched Captain Blade. He drew himself up, staring ahead without an expression on his face. He looked strangely pale under his dark beard. Sam knew it couldn't be fear but what was it?

"No, I'll not be staining the planks of me new ship with your lily-livered blood," growled Blackheart. "I'm taking the *Sea Wolf* to Puerto Caballo where there's plenty of rich men who'll buy her from me. Think on that, Blade. Your ship will be some landlubber lord's plaything."

Blade's fists clenched. "You'll regret this, Blackheart!" he cried. "You haven't seen the last of me and my brave lads."

Blackheart threw back his head and gave a resounding laugh. "Oh, I think I have. Set up planks," he ordered his crew. "Find as many as you can that'll serve the purpose. I'm not wasting any more time on this scum."

Five lengths of wood were quickly found and lashed over the side of the ship.

Fernando leaned close to Sam. "That blaggard would never have succeeded if we hadn't fallen ill." He cursed under his breath in Spanish. "It was Peter's barnacle stew that did for us. Well done for missing that meal."

So that was why Blackheart had been able to take the ship so easily. The crew were ill with food poisoning! Sam remembered his last trip to the past. With perfect timing the coin had whisked him off home just as the foul-smelling stew was being served. It was always good to miss Peter's dreadful cooking, but this time he'd been doubly lucky!

Sam felt himself being pushed roughly forwards. As he stood behind Fernando, ready to take his turn to plunge into the sea, he had a sudden thought that almost made his heart stop. Charlie had never learned to swim! He scanned the faces of his crewmates and a horrible fear twisted his insides. Charlie was already on one of the planks. Pale and trembling, she was fighting the man who was forcing her towards the drop.

"Someone help Charlie!" he yelled. The *Sea Wolf* pirates tried to go to her aid, but Blackheart's men held them all back, laughing cruelly.

"Don't make me jump!" screamed Charlie. "I'll drown."

There was a fresh gale of laughter at this.

"What's all the fuss?" said Blackheart, pushing everyone aside to get to her. "Are my crew being unkind to a poor young pirate?"

Charlie gulped. "Take pity on me, sir," she whispered. "I've never learned to swim."

"I'll jump with Charlie!" shouted Sam, trying to break free and get to her.

Blackheart shook his head. He stepped up onto the plank. "No need for that," he said pleasantly. "I'm always ready to help when help be needed."

Sam saw Charlie's look of relief at his words. But in an instant it was wiped off her face as Blackheart swept her up under one arm and stormed to the end of the plank.

"I'll help you to your death!" he growled, as he tossed her into the ocean. "Now, who's volunteering to go next?"

"Me!" yelled Sam, wrenching himself free and fighting his way to the nearest plank.

He took it at a run and launched himself into the sea. He kicked hard and surfaced, his eyes feverishly searching the waves. There was no sign of Charlie. And then the water swirled and she burst into view, her arms flailing as she tried to keep afloat. Spluttering and coughing, she disappeared below the swell again.

Sam swam faster than he'd ever swum before. The water churned ahead – Charlie was fighting for her life but she was losing the battle. Sam briefly saw the panic on her face before she vanished. He sucked in a huge breath and dived after her.

Charlie wasn't struggling now. Her body was slowly sinking to the seabed. Sam took hold of her jerkin and kicked upwards, tugging with what strength he had left. But Charlie was a dead weight, pulling him down. Sam's lungs were screaming for air, and the surface didn't seem to be getting any closer.

After what felt like hours but he knew could only be seconds, Sam finally burst above the waves, gulping in air. He looked into Charlie's face. She lay there, lifeless.

Was he too late?

CHAPTER FOUR

Suddenly Charlie took in a ragged breath, coughing and spluttering as she spat salty water from her lungs.

"What's going on?" she shrieked, lashing out. Sam seized her arms.

"What's going on is that I'm trying to save your life!" he told her. "So stop struggling and let me get on with it."

He pushed her onto her back, clamped

his hand firmly round her chin and towed her towards the island. "And no arguing."

At last they reached the hard, rocky shore. They pulled themselves out of the sea and lay on a flat rock, gasping.

"Thanks for getting me here!" panted Charlie. "I don't think I was much help."

"You weren't," said Sam with a grin. "You're lucky we made it. The only other time I've ever done that was in a lesson at my local swimming pool with a lifeguard standing by . . ."

"Shh!" warned Charlie. "One of the

others might hear your strange talk."

Sam was always forgetting that he mustn't use modern words in front of the crew. They'd never understand that he came from three hundred years in the future.

All around, the *Sea Wolf* pirates were stumbling from the waves. Sam raised his head and gazed back at their ship. He felt sick as he saw the sails catch the wind. Blackheart and his men were stealing her and there was nothing Sam could do to stop them.

"We'll win her back," whispered Charlie.

"Too right," agreed Sam, anger bubbling up inside him. "That fiend's not getting away with it."

Harry Hopp stumbled towards them, his peg leg catching on the harsh stones. He was searching every face and counting out loud.

"We're all here, Captain," he called at last. "Everyone accounted for."

He flopped down onto a rock. Sam could see that the whole crew looked pale and exhausted.

"It's a blessing we survived," Blade called back. "And we can thank Sam for keeping Charlie alive."

The pirates gave a ragged cheer.

"Has anyone seen Sinbad?" Charlie asked suddenly.

"Or Crow?" added Sam, casting desperately about for the ship's cat and parrot. He knew Sinbad could take care of himself, but why hadn't Crow flown to the island to be with the crew?

"Don't fret," said Ned, patting Charlie's shoulder. "We'd have heard if Blackheart had tried to make old Sinbad walk the plank. He'd have caused a right royal fuss. And Crow's squawks would wake the dead."

"I bet they've hidden somewhere and are giving that scurvy lot a hard time right now," said Fernando.

"I never thought Blackheart would defeat us," groaned Ben.

Captain Blade jumped to his feet. Sam could see he was shaking with rage. "That villain would never have got the better of us if we'd been well," he growled. "Just wait until I get my hands on him."

Peter raised a trembling finger. "You won't be able to do that, Captain," he said mournfully. "We're marooned here. We're all going to die."

"By Jupiter!" thundered Captain Blade. "We're not staying here to perish. We're going after our ship."

"Yay!" cried Sam, but the rest of the crew just gawped at the captain.

"He's talking like a madman," whispered Ned.

"The sea water's got into his brain," muttered Peter.

"Begging your pardon, sir," said Ben nervously, "but how are we going to do that? We haven't got a boat."

Blade strode up and down the rocky shore, staring fiercely out at the horizon where the *Sea Wolf* was fast disappearing. He tugged angrily at the red braids in his beard.

"We'll build a boat," he declared. "We just need wood."

Sam surveyed the rocky island. It wasn't a very hopeful sight. There was one scrubby tree in the distance — hardly enough wood for a deckchair.

Blade stared into the bleak faces of his men.

"We're not giving up," he said through gritted teeth. "We can't let the *Sea Wolf* down."

Sam went to his side and faced the crew. "The captain's right," he called. "There has to be a way."

"I'm willing to help," said Charlie.

"Well said!" called Fernando.

"We may be weak, but we are not defeated!" thundered the captain. "Stand up, my brave crew, and join me."

Fernando and Charlie were first to their feet. Ned and Ben followed, with Harry Hopp clumping close behind. The others looked at their leader with bewildered eyes.

"I thought all my men were loyal to the *Sea Wolf!*" declared Blade, pacing round them, his eyes blazing. "Are we going to let that villain take her?"

"No!" came the cry.

"Then we must go after the blaggard!"

"We'll get our vessel back!" shouted Fernando.

"Long live the *Sea Wolf!*" yelled the pirates. Sam thought they still looked green about the gills, but now there was hope in their eyes again.

"Let's get hunting for timber," said Ben eagerly.

"And we'll find food and water at the same time," said Harry Hopp. "But look sharp. It'll be dark soon."

"If only we had a tarpaulin," said Fernando, "we could catch the dew overnight."

"That's right," Sam burst out. "I saw how to do it on the Internet once and . . ." He broke off as he realised everyone was staring at him. *Oops,* he thought, *the Internet hasn't been invented yet!* "No, silly me," he gabbled, "you wouldn't catch dew *in a net.* The water would all spill through."

Fernando shook his head. "You may be my good friend," he said, "but you do say some strange things sometimes."

The captain split the crew into search parties and sent them in different directions. Sam set off eastward along the rocky shore with Fernando and Charlie. They kept their eyes peeled for signs of food or wood that had been washed up by the tide.

Sam knelt by a small patch of limpets. "We could eat these," he said, pulling at the hard shells with his fingers, trying to prise them from the rock.

"Don't waste your time," said Fernando. "You'd need a knife and Blackheart's scurvy seadogs have got all our weapons."

"I wouldn't want them anyway," grinned Charlie, holding her tummy. "I've only just got over Peter's barnacle stew!"

They clambered round a headland.

"Wow!" gasped Sam, stopping short.

A wrecked ship lay abandoned on the rocks, the mainmast snapped in two. Sam could just make out the painted name – *Lady Eliza.* More shattered vessels were scattered on the shore beyond.

Charlie shuddered. "Looks like a ships' graveyard," she said in a low voice.

"I think we've found our wood supply,

though," said Sam, running up and pulling at a plank that hung from a gaping hole in the *Eliza's* hull.

As the plank came away in his hands there was a clatter above. Sam looked up to find himself face to face with a human skull!

CHAPTER FIVE

The eyeless sockets stared right at Sam. Now he could see the whole skeleton dangling from the wreck. Its bones gleamed in the last rays of the sun.

"Well, there's not a lot of hope for us on this island," said Fernando, with a feeble laugh. "*He* doesn't seem to have found any food."

"The sooner we leave, the better," said

Charlie, backing off. "Let's bring the captain and show him all this wood."

Ned's eyes lit up when he and the captain arrived to see the *Lady Eliza*. "Well, I'll be a smoked kipper," he declared, rubbing his chin. "This tub can be repaired – although it'll take time."

"And time's something we haven't got!" said the captain impatiently. "What about those other wrecks? Have we the makings of a raft?"

"Aye!" said Ned. "There's plenty of planks here – and rope enough to lash them together. I'll warrant we could build a small craft in a day. But it would only hold about seven men."

"Then seven men will go after the *Sea Wolf*," said the captain, thumping his fist in his hand.

"That will be enough," cried Fernando. "We're the best pirates in the Caribbean."

Blade slapped him on the back. "Well said, lad. Let's get to it!"

The pirates worked hard through the night, their stomachs growling with hunger. Peter had managed to catch a couple of fish and cook them over a small fire, but the crew had only got a mouthful each.

"Never mind," said Sam cheerfully when they complained. "You being hungry is good news!"

"How do you work that out, my friend?" asked Fernando, giving him a puzzled look. "It's not a nice feeling."

"But you must be getting over Peter's

stew," Sam explained. "My mum always says 'If you can eat, you must be feeling better'."

By the light of the moon, the pirates found a few rusty tools still lying in one of the wrecks. Ned set some of the men to work, lashing planks together to form the solid base of a raft. Ben took a long wooden yard that had once held up a mainsail and fixed it into the rough deck

as a mast. A smaller one was tied at right angles near the top and a tattered sail now hung from it.

Fernando appeared with three long oars. "They're a bit splintered but they'll do," he said, showing the crew. "Two to row and one for the rudder."

Sam looked up from where he and Charlie were tying jagged pieces of conch shell to short lengths of wood to make weapons. Dawn was breaking over the eastern horizon, bathing everything in a pale yellow light. They'd be setting sail soon. He hoped he'd be one of the raft crew.

"Shiver me timbers," said Harry Hopp, rubbing his rough chin as he wove rowlocks out of rope and fixed them to the raft to hold the oars in place. "I hope that pitiful sail will catch the wind, for it's all we could find."

"Aye, our craft is a bit like us," said

Ben, with a wry smile. "Rough round the edges!"

"As long as she floats, she'll get us there," said Captain Blade. "Make sure we take any spare rope we can find, in case we need to make repairs."

"What are we going to call her?" asked Charlie.

"That's right," said Fernando. "She's got to have a name after all our hard work."

Ned chuckled and rubbed his sore hands. "How about the *Sweat and Splinters?*"

"The *Last Hope,*" suggested Harry Hopp.

"I've got it," cried Sam. "We're out to recover the *Sea Wolf* and pay Blackheart back, so what about the *Wolf's Revenge?*"

"That's a fine name!" exclaimed the captain, his eyes blazing. "The *Wolf's Revenge* it is."

"Aye!" cried the crew.

"And who's going to sail on this magnificent craft?" asked Harry.

"Not you, that's for sure!" said Ben. "You'd get your peg leg stuck between the planks."

"Stap me!" laughed Harry. "You'll be swabbing the decks for that when we get back on the *Sea Wolf*!"

"Ben, Peter, you're on the raft with me," said the captain. "And Ned – you know the lie of the land at Puerto Caballo."

He looked keenly from one man to another. Sam could see that everyone wanted to go with the captain to reclaim their beloved ship. He hoped his name would be called. He could just picture the scene . . . Blackheart and his evil crew cowering before the brave men of the *Sea Wolf* with their vicious shells on sticks.

He snapped out of his daydream to see Ned and Ben pushing the *Wolf's Revenge* into the shallows and jumping on board. Charlie and Fernando were joining them. Were they going without him?

"Look lively, Sam!" called the captain,

wading out to the raft. "We need you and your wily Silver ways."

Sam bounded eagerly onto the makeshift craft and sat cross-legged beside his friends. His name must have been called while he was whacking the imaginary enemy with conch shells.

The captain took his hat off and gave a solemn bow to Harry Hopp and the other pirates left on shore. "Harry – you're in charge. We'll be back for you all in the twitch of a rat's whisker."

The men cheered as the ragged sail filled with wind and the *Wolf's Revenge* bobbed over the waves towards the open sea.

Suddenly there was a flutter of green feathers and Crow landed on Blade's head. "All aboard!" he squawked. The captain froze, a look of horror on his face.

"Crow!" cried Sam, quickly untangling the parrot from the captain's hair. "You escaped!"

"Reporting for duty," chirped Crow.

"Keep that bird away from me," said Blade faintly.

Captain Blade, bravest man on the seas, had just one fear — parrots. Ben said it was because one had pecked him on the nose when he was a baby. But all the pirates had a different story to tell. Crow was only allowed to stay aboard the ship if everybody pretended he was just a crow — a talking crow with green feathers!

Charlie stroked Crow under the chin. "If only he could tell us that Sinbad's okay."

"Don't worry," Fernando reassured her. "He'll be terrorising Blackheart's men as we speak."

Charlie nodded and gave a small smile.

"Keep the sun to port," ordered the captain, turning his back on the parrot. "We're heading south for Hispaniola — and Puerto Caballo."

The sun rose in the sky, beating down on them as the hours passed. The wind died and Ben rolled up the sail and took over rowing duty with Peter. The captain stood at the mast, his face set and determined.

Fernando gazed at the vast expanse of empty water. "Rowing's too slow," he muttered to Sam. "At this rate the *Sea Wolf* will be sold long before we reach the port."

"Don't let Captain Blade hear you," warned Charlie. "Look at him. There's only one thing on his mind – getting his ship back."

No sooner had she spoken than the surface of the water suddenly erupted and the raft began to rock dangerously. The crew threw themselves flat, clutching the sides. Crow fluttered into the air with a frightened squawk.

"Something hit the raft!" called Ned in

alarm. "It knocked the rudder clean out of my hand!"

Sam stared in horror at the swirling sea. All around them the waves heaved, throwing up blinding spray. The *Wolf's Revenge* was buffeted from side to side. A moaning, howling sound filled the air. The pirates clung in fear to the raft as it began to rise out of the water.

CHAPTER SIX

The *Wolf's Revenge* heaved and bucked, the timbers grinding against each other, threatening to burst their ropes. Sam saw Charlie lose her grip. He shot out an arm and hooked his fingers round her belt before she could tumble overboard.

"Thank you!" she spluttered, scrabbling at the wet planks. "What's going on?"

The strange trumpeting cry was all around them now.

"A sea monster's got us," wailed Peter.

"Could be mermaids," croaked Ben, hanging by one hand from the mast.

"Those she-devils would drown a sailor soon as look at him!" cried Ned.

"Stop your jabbering!" shouted Captain Blade. "Save your strength to hold on."

The raft was suddenly tossed in the air. As it slammed back down on the water, Sam caught sight of a huge fanned tail disappearing under the surface. He peered over the side. The sea was full of sleek

grey-black creatures swimming slowly below them, each one longer than a bus.

"They're whales!" he cried in excitement. "And that trumpeting sound is whalesong!"

"I don't know why you're so pleased," shouted Fernando. "They're common enough round here. And this lot are trying to capsize us!"

Sam knew he couldn't tell the crew, but whales didn't visit Backwater Bay and he'd never seen one so close before. It was awesome and scary at the same time. He gazed at the magnificent creatures. Their skin was grooved and shining and their flippers were as big as surfboards.

"Man the oars," came the captain's order. "Let's get clear of them quickly."

"Just one more coming and then they'll be gone," said Peter, looking to the stern.

"They seem to be heading for Hispaniola," said Charlie wistfully as Ben and Fernando began rowing again. "I wish we could go that fast."

A brilliant idea came full sail into Sam's brain. "We *could* go that fast!" he burst out. "I once sat in a wheelie bin while my friend rode his bike and towed me along on the end of a rope—" Charlie coughed loudly and Sam realised that the crew were scratching their heads. No one knew what he was talking about. "I mean . . . if we tie a rope round a whale's tail, it'll tow us along."

"Excellent plan, Sam!" said the captain. "That beast is one of the strongest creatures in the ocean. It won't notice the weight of our puny raft."

"Never heard such nonsense!" muttered Peter. "Once it reaches its feeding ground it'll dive for sure, pulling us under and drowning us all!"

But the captain was already tying a length of rope to the raft, leaving a loose end on the knot for a quick release. "Avast your whingeing! We have to take that risk if we want to get to our ship in time."

"The moment we see the front whales dive we'll untether ourselves," added Ned.

Fernando took the free end of the rope and tied a slip knot in it, leaving a huge loop. "Leave it to me," he said. "I can throw a rope around a mooring post with my eyes closed."

"Mooring posts don't move!" laughed Charlie. "You'd better keep your eyes open this time."

"It won't work," said Peter gloomily.

"Watch this!" said Fernando. The rope snaked out high over the water, the stiff loop keeping its shape. It landed over one fluke of a whale's tail and Fernando immediately gave it a sharp twist that sent a judder through it.

To the astonishment of his companions, the loop flicked up and over the whole tail, tightening as the weight of the raft pulled the rope taut.

At once the *Wolf's Revenge* sped up, cutting through the water. The pirates were thrown backwards and clung together to keep their balance. The whale swam off, with the raft bucking and bouncing after it. It reminded Sam of being on Terrorwave at his local theme park, but he remembered just in time not to say that out loud.

For what seemed like hours all Sam could see was the empty ocean stretching ahead and the whales ploughing along, lashing their tails on the surface.

Then, as they crested a large swell, he spotted something in the far distance. A green coastline was coming into view, a forested mountain rising above.

"Land ho!" he called.

"That's Hispaniola all right," said Ned cheerfully. "See that headland? That's Columbus Point. Puerto Caballo will be in sight soon."

The crew gave a cheer but Charlie shouted in alarm. "The whales are diving. They've reached their feeding ground!"

"We must release our tow line," cried Ned. He felt for the end of the rope and gave it a tug. Nothing happened. The knot was caught between the planks. "It's stuck, Captain."

"And the whale's going down to feed any second!" yelled Peter.

Without a word, Captain Blade threw off his hat and coat and dived into the water. He surfaced and pulled himself along the rope towards the whale.

"He's going to try and untie it!" gasped Sam.

"He'll never get near!" said Charlie.

But now the captain was on the whale's

back, pulling at the knot. The huge
creature thrashed about so violently that
Sam was sure he'd be thrown into the sea
at any minute.

"He's loosened the rope," gasped
Fernando.

"He's running out of time," said Ben.
"The other whales have already gone."

With that the whale's back heaved above
the waves in a smooth arc. It let out a
huge spout of water and dived below the
surface, its tail flicking high in the air. The
captain was thrown aside and vanished
into the churning sea.

"We're going down!" cried Peter.

"Abandon ship!" screeched Crow.

Suddenly the raft lurched to a stop. The
pirates fell backwards with a jolt.

"He's untied the rope!" exclaimed Sam.
"The captain's saved us!" He scrambled
to his knees. "But what's happened to
him?"

The whales had disappeared and
the water was calm. Captain Blade was
nowhere to be seen. The sea had swallowed
him up.

CHAPTER SEVEN

"The captain's drowned," groaned Peter.
"He can't have," cried Sam. "I'll
dive in and search."

"It's too dangerous with those huge
creatures around," said Ned, sorrowfully.
Head bowed, he began to pull in the tow
rope.

The water in front of him suddenly
heaved and a head appeared.

"By Davy Jones!" came the ringing voice of the captain. "You're a miserable-looking bunch."

"You're alive!" squealed Charlie, nearly falling overboard as she helped him onto the raft.

Blade shook himself like a dog and turned a beaming face on the open-mouthed crew.

"You saved us all," declared Sam.

"We thought you'd drowned," added Peter.

"I haven't got time for drowning," said Captain Blade. "I've got a ship to rescue. The wind's up so get that sail trimmed and start rowing!"

As they neared land Sam could see a port ahead, with a stone jetty jutting out into the sea, and buildings of all shapes and sizes clustered around the water's edge.

"I recall there's an inlet to the west, Captain," Ned told him. "We could go ashore there and make for the town on foot."

The captain nodded solemnly. "And I pray we're not too late."

The *Sea Wolf* pirates were soon on land, leaving their raft among rocks in the deserted inlet and making for the track that led along the coast. The sun was still high in the sky as Captain Blade called them to a halt at a crossroads. The fingerpost pointed over a wooden bridge to Puerto Caballo, just a quarter of a mile away.

"What's the plan, Captain?" asked Ben.

"Sam, you go into town to find out what's happening to my ship," ordered Blade. "A young lad like you will pass among the townsfolk more easily than us weather-beaten buccaneers. Fernando, you go too. Most people here speak Spanish." He looked earnestly into their faces. "I know you won't let me down."

"We won't, Captain," said Sam, swelling with pride. "The *Sea Wolf* means the world to us."

"But remember," Blade went on, "while you're keeping out of Blackheart's sight, don't forget to hide from the governor's men too. There's nothing they like more than stringing up a few pirates."

Fernando laughed. "At least Blackheart won't be expecting us. He thinks we're busy killing each other on that accursed island."

"He does that," agreed Blade bitterly. "So lie low and report back here as soon as you can. The . . . crow had better stay with us," he added reluctantly. "He'll only give you away."

Sam coaxed Crow onto Charlie's shoulder. Then he and Fernando ran off down the track. Soon it widened into a road and they passed cottages with small pens where animals grazed. They headed for the tumble of buildings that made up the port town.

"Down to the harbour first," said
Fernando. "We've got to see if our ship's
still there."

"This way," Sam replied. "I can see
masts beyond the church tower."

They stopped at the harbour wall. Sam
hardly dared look at the vessels that lay at
anchor. Suppose the *Sea Wolf* wasn't there?
The port was full of bobbing ships and
boats, but none that looked familiar.

"There's a vessel moored along the jetty,"
exclaimed Sam suddenly. "I can only see
the stern between the two galleons in front
of it, but I'd swear that's the *Sea Wolf*."

They sauntered along the jetty and
the side of the ship came into full view.
There were the three lanterns rising from
the poop deck, the wooden crow's nest
like a barrel perched on top of the main
mast, and Sam almost gave a cry as he
spotted the figurehead — the face of a

snarling wolf. He caught Fernando's arm in excitement. "It *is* the *Sea Wolf*!"

"She could be sold already," said Fernando in a low voice.

"Let's check it out," whispered Sam.

"Wait! Don't go any closer," Fernando whispered back. "I can see one of Blackheart's men guarding her. She's not been sold yet. She's still in his thieving hands."

"How are we going to discover what his plans are?" muttered Sam as they made their way back along the jetty.

"We need to ask around," said Fernando. "But we'll have to be careful how we do it."

Two sailors sat on the harbour wall. Sam could hear they were speaking in English, so he went over.

"I've got a message for a Captain Smith," he said, pointing to the *Sea Wolf*. "Is that his ship?"

The older man shrugged. "Never seen her before."

"Me neither," said the other, turning away.

Fernando nodded towards a group of young children playing skittles on the square. They were calling to each other in Spanish. "Let's try our luck with them," he said. "They're sure to have noticed if an ugly cove with an eye patch went past."

The children stopped their game as Fernando called to them in their language. He gathered up all the skittles and began to juggle expertly.

The children jostled round, watching and chattering to him in high-pitched voices.

"No luck," Fernando called to Sam, without taking his eyes off the skittles. "Where can we try next?"

A small hand tugged at Sam's jerkin. A little girl gabbled away in Spanish, her eyes growing wide with fright as she told her tale.

"She says she saw a stranger go into that tavern there," Fernando translated. "He was 'talking foreign' to a sailor that she

knows. She said the stranger was dressed
like a sea captain and he had a scary face."

"Sounds like Blackheart," Sam replied.
"Must have been speaking English. I'll slip
in there and see what's going on."

It was gloomy inside the busy inn. The
small, dirty windows barely let in the sun.
Sam slunk round, keeping to the dark
corners. Blackheart was easy to spot. He
stood at the bar, rocking back on his heels,
a tankard in his hand. He was telling
another man that he'd come to Puerto

Caballo to sell the finest ship in all the seas.

"How much would you be wanting for her, Mr . . . er . . . ?" asked his companion, looking interested.

"Mr Black," said the pirate captain. "But you're too late. She's sold already. I'm just waiting for the gentleman to come with me gold." He thumped his tankard down on the bar, making Sam jump. "More rum!" he demanded.

"Who's buying the vessel?" asked the sailor, edging his glass close to Blackheart's in the hope of getting a free drink.

"His name's Oliver Castle," Blackheart told him. "I've not had the pleasure of meeting him yet. He kept me waiting for over a day to say yay or nay."

His thirsty friend nodded. "He's the richest gent on the island and spends money like it was water. Every year he adds another wing to his house at La Isabella.

Looks more like a palace than a home."

"That figures," said Blackheart, downing his rum in one. "I had a message saying he'd been detained at home by his builders. But he'll be here at four o'clock and we'll complete the deal."

"You can't miss him, Mr Black," laughed the sailor, turning to leave. "He's got the only gold coach on the island!"

Sam wanted to whoop. Spying was easier than it looked. He'd only been there a few minutes and he'd got all the information the crew needed! In his hurry to get to the door he bumped into a woman collecting tankards. She dropped them with a clatter, cursing him for his clumsiness.

"Sorry," mumbled Sam, trying to slip past her.

"Hold hard, boy," came a rasping voice. It was Blackheart. He'd spotted Sam!

CHAPTER EIGHT

Blackheart seized Sam's wrist with iron fingers and pulled him into a shadowy corner.

"I know you," he hissed. "You're *Sea Wolf* scum!" He tightened his grip, twisting Sam's arm so hard Sam thought it would break. "How did you get off that island?" he snapped. "Did anyone else escape?"

"No!" croaked Sam, hardly able to

breathe with the pain. "I came here on my own. My name's Sam and I'm the only survivor."

Blackheart slowly loosened his grip. "I hope you're telling me the truth, boy," he snarled. "Do you know what happens to those who lie to Blackheart?" He drew a finger across his throat.

Sam gulped. "Surely no one would dare lie to the greatest pirate ever to sail the oceans," he said nervously.

Blackheart nodded smugly. "Well said,

Sam. Now tell me what happened to Blade and his bunch of good-for-nothings."

"It was awful on that island," said Sam with a shudder. He hoped he was acting well enough to convince their evil enemy. "It was like you said it would be. The crew didn't stick together and in the end they . . ."

Blackheart let out a laugh of pure evil. "They killed each other! Just as I thought!"

"I escaped on a raft." Sam went on.

Blackheart's eyes narrowed with distrust. "You got here very quickly if you were on a raft," he growled.

"I got a bit of a tow on the way," explained Sam. "And I came to find you, Captain Blackheart," he added quickly.

"I'm Mr Black here," snarled the pirate.

"Sorry, sir," said Sam. "I never wanted to join the *Sea Wolf* crew. They kidnapped me. I couldn't believe my luck when you captured us so cleverly . . ."

"Then why did you try to attack me?" asked Blackheart suspiciously.

Oh dear, thought Sam. *I'd forgotten that little detail.* "I couldn't just stride up and say 'Well done, sir!' could I?" he said boldly. "That would have given the game away and my shipmates would have killed me once we got to the island. I had to pretend to be on their side, didn't I? Anyway, I'd never have hurt you. You're my hero, sir. Stealing the *Sea Wolf* and then deciding not to scupper her but sell her instead — that was a brilliant plan! Do say you'll let me join your crew." He gave the villain a pleading look.

Blackheart stroked his beard. "You're a bright boy, Sam, and I can see you're different from a lot of young 'uns."

Sam stifled a laugh. *He's right about that*, he thought. *Little does he know* how *different*.

"I be short-handed at present," continued the pirate. "Some of my crew

had to man the *Grinning*— I mean, my
ship. And the *Sea Wolf* needs her decks
scrubbing so she's shipshape and ready
for sale." He rubbed his hands in glee.
"Castle should be here with his bags of
gold within the hour. If you want to join
me you'd better get to work!" He looked
hard at Sam. "What's the matter, boy? You
weren't expecting to be first mate straight
off, were you?"

"Of course not, Captain— Mr Black,"
gabbled Sam, thinking furiously. If he
couldn't get back to his friends and tell
them about the buyer before he started
scrubbing the decks, the *Sea Wolf* would be
sold and gone! But how could he do it?
Then it came to him. "I'm happy to do
anything, sir, but there's one person I must
tell the good news to first."

"No time for that!" snapped the pirate
captain. He settled down in a chair and
called for more rum. "Be off with you."

"But I have to let my mother know," pleaded Sam. "She'll be so pleased for me."

Unbelievably, Blackheart's evil face appeared to soften. "Of course, lad. Good boy for thinking of her. Don't be long now."

It works every time, thought Sam in relief. *There's nothing pirates love more than their mothers.*

He marched boldly out of the tavern, hoping Fernando was still around – but there was no sign of him. He must have realised that something was wrong when Sam was so long in the tavern and rushed back to the crossroads to warn the others. Sam decided to go there as quickly as he could to tell them what he'd found out. But he didn't have long. Blackheart would expect to see him on the *Sea Wolf* when the buyer turned up.

As he walked along a quiet cobbled street he heard footsteps behind him. Sam stopped. The footsteps stopped. Sam walked on and heard the footsteps

again. When he spun round he saw a
shabby man with a hat pulled low over
his face, mooching along after him. The
man immediately ducked into an alley but
Sam caught a quick glimpse of his face.
His blood ran cold. It was Hooknose!
Blackheart must have sent him to follow
Sam and make sure he was really going to
see his mother. And his mum
was three hundred years
away!

CHAPTER NINE

Sam had to shake off his pursuer. He sped up and the footsteps quickened behind him. As he turned into another street he saw a woman ahead, carrying a basket of fruit. Sam ran up to her and caught her arm.

"There's a nasty man after me," he sobbed. "I'm so scared. If you pretend to be my mother I think he'll go away."

The woman put down her basket
and rolled up her sleeves. For a second
Sam thought she was going to chase *him*
away. But she turned in fury to confront
Hooknose. "Be off, you scoundrel!" she
shrieked, storming towards him. "Leave
my son alone." A look of terror came over
the man's face and he fled.

"Thank you!" breathed Sam gratefully.
He might not be so good at spying, after
all, but he was proud of his acting! Maybe
he'd join the drama club at school when he
got back to the twenty-first century.

"Don't mention it, my dear!" said the woman, pressing an apple into Sam's hand. "Now, you be careful."

Sam looked round. There was no sign of Hooknose. He sprinted off towards the crossroads to find his crew.

The *Sea Wolf* pirates came running out from the trees with huge smiles on their faces when they saw Sam. Crow flapped over to his shoulder and buried his head in his neck.

"We haven't got much time," Sam told the crew. "I heard Blackheart boasting that he has a buyer for the *Sea Wolf*, and the man's coming for her at four o'clock."

The crew muttered angrily at this.

"Who is it?" asked Captain Blade.

"Some gentleman called Oliver Castle," said Sam. "He lives at La Isabella."

"Oliver Castle!"

Charlie spat out the name as if it was poison. Sam could see that she'd turned pale.

"You know him?" asked Fernando.

Charlie nodded. "He's a friend of my stepfather."

Ben patted her shoulder. "Then he's no friend of ours!" he growled.

"Scurvy sea scum!" squawked Crow.

"For once I have to agree with that bird," said the captain angrily. "I'd rather see our ship at the bottom of the ocean than in the hands of someone like that."

Charlie was due to inherit a lot of money from her dead mother when she was twenty-one. But her stepfather had a different idea. He'd wanted Charlie to make a will, leaving all her money to him, and then he'd planned to kill her so that he could have the loot straight away. Luckily for Charlie, she'd run away to the protection of Captain Blade and his crew.

"What do you know of this Castle?" asked the captain.

"He's one of the richest men on Hispaniola," said Charlie. "And he'll do anything to make money. He spends it freely too and he takes his son, Augustus, with him. Augustus is so spoilt that it wouldn't surprise me if Castle was buying the *Sea Wolf* as a plaything for him."

"What do we do?" asked Peter. "The easiest thing would be to wait till she's sold and then take her back by force from this Castle."

"But there's no revenge in that!" declared Fernando fiercely. "Blackheart will have sailed away a rich man."

"I will have my revenge," growled Captain Blade. "No one steals my ship and gets away with it."

"Or throws me in the sea!" added Charlie.

"We could ambush Castle," suggested

Ned. "He can't buy our ship if he doesn't turn up."

"But maybe Castle *should* buy the ship," Sam burst out, his brain whirring. He realised that the crew were gawping at him so he quickly told them the idea that had sprung into his head like a kangaroo. "We ambush him but then we take his coach and the money and one of us pretends to *be* him and does the deal with Blackheart."

Captain Blade thought about this for a moment and then slapped Sam on the back. "By the stars, lad, that's a splendid idea!"

"We'll just have to hope Blackheart doesn't recognise us," said Ned.

"He didn't see my face," Ben put in. "That barnacle stew had me doubled up in pain all the time he was on board."

"But what about our weapons?" asked Peter. "We've only got shells on sticks."

"If we take them by surprise, we won't have to fight," declared the captain. "Now where shall we stage our ambush?"

"La Isabella is five miles west of here," said Ned. "So Castle will be coming along this very road."

Blade checked the position of the sun. "And they'll have to pass soon if they're to get to Blackheart by four," he said. "Sam, Ned, Fernando, get up that overhanging tree. When they slow for the bridge, drop on them. The rest of us will attack from down here."

"I can't stay!" gasped Sam. "I've just remembered. I've joined Blackheart's crew! I've got to get to the *Sea Wolf* and scrub the decks."

The pirates looked at him in shock. He quickly explained what had happened.

"If I don't get there soon," he finished, "he'll know that I've been lying to him. He'll suspect that I wasn't the only one who escaped from the island."

"No time," said the captain urgently.

"I hear hooves. Get to your positions."

"It's not a coach!" cried Fernando, who had already climbed the tree. "It's soldiers. Governor's men!"

"Quick! Everyone hide in the reeds under the bridge," ordered the captain, as Fernando hastily swung back down to the ground. "If they find us, they'll know we're buccaneers."

Sam knew what that meant. They'd be for the gallows!

There was only just enough space for them all to cram onto the narrow bank underneath the bridge. Sam could hear the thud of hooves as the horses came nearer. He tensed, waiting for the thunderous noise they'd make on the wooden planks of the bridge, but it didn't come. Instead he heard the scuffing of stones being kicked up as the horses came to a halt. A commanding voice rapped out some words in Spanish.

"The men are being ordered to search,"

whispered Fernando, translating for the
crew. "Their leader's telling them to
cover every inch of ground,
including the stream. I
think they're on to us."

CHAPTER TEN

Through the long rushes Sam saw figures striding around, their heads bent as they thrust their musket barrels into the reeds.

"Any chance of running away when they're not looking?" whispered Peter.

"Only if you want a bullet in your back," muttered Blade.

The pirates sank lower into their hiding

place. The leader up on the bank bellowed out an order.

"They're not looking for us," hissed Fernando. "The sergeant has lost something. He thinks it happened this morning when they stopped here to water their horses."

He listened as the officer spoke again. "It's a money pouch," he translated. "And they're not leaving till they've found it."

"Then they'll find us first," whispered Charlie, horrified. "What are we going to do?"

There was a sudden shower of loose earth, and black boots came into view. Someone was sliding towards the water.

The pirates shrank further back as the soldier began prodding the reeds with his musket. Each step was bringing him closer.

Sam suddenly remembered something he'd seen in a film. A boy spy had tricked his pursuers by throwing a marble to make

a sound behind them and so distract them
from his hiding place. Sam felt about
for a stone. His fingers closed around
something lumpy. It was a pouch, muddy
and dripping. This must be what the
troops were looking for!

Thud! The musket hit the ground only
inches from Sam's leg. He had to act now!

He slowly stretched out his hand through
the thick reeds and dropped the pouch
onto the man's boot. The soldier paused,
ears pricked. Sam felt his crewmates tense
behind him. He held his breath.

The man stooped, pushing the reeds aside. He gave a cry of surprise. Had he seen them? But the next minute he'd snatched up the pouch and was holding it above his head.

He climbed the slippery bank, yelling in delight. With a burst of excited Spanish the soldiers left.

Cautiously the pirates climbed back to the road. Fernando shinned up the overhanging tree once more to watch them disappear round a distant bend in the road.

"Saved by Sam's quick thinking!" said Captain Blade. "Well done, lad."

"I second that!" said Ben. "Those soldiers came so close I thought—"

Fernando gave a sudden shout. "There's a gold coach coming from La Isabella! It must be Castle."

"To your places!" commanded Blade. "Sam, you'll be going back to town in style!"

From his place next to Fernando on the high branch, Sam watched the coach throwing up dust as it rumbled along the rough road. Even from a distance it was an amazing sight, glinting with gold paint and pulled by gleaming white horses, peacock feathers on their bridles. Every inch of the coach was covered in ornate golden dolphins, lions and dragons, all showing a lot of teeth. It reminded Sam of Fat Frank who roared around Backwater Bay in a bright yellow sports car with a sticker that said 'Megadriver' and a horn that frightened old ladies.

"There's someone next to the driver," muttered Ned in a warning voice. "He's got a gun."

"You and I'll take him," said Fernando grimly. "We'll leave the driver to you, Sam. He's so blubbery he won't be able to put up a fight."

Sam, Fernando and Ned shrank back

among the dense leaves. Sam's heart was racing, knuckles white as he gripped the branch he was crouching on. They had to get this ambush right first time and it wasn't going to be easy. Oliver Castle's coach was still charging along. It looked as if it was going to take the bridge at top speed.

"Whoa!" called the driver suddenly and the horses slowed. The coach approached the bridge at a sedate trot, passing just below the pirates.

"Now!" hissed Fernando.

He and Ned dropped silently onto the gunman's back, knocking the rifle from his hand. Sam leapt after them, crashing into the driver who was so shocked he pulled the reins sharply and the horses jolted to a halt. Sam heard cries of fear as his shipmates swarmed into the coach brandishing their weapons.

With lightning speed, Fernando whipped off his captive's neckerchief and

used it to tie his hands behind his back. With a whoop of joy, he found a knife in the man's pocket and stuck it in his belt.

"Don't hurt me!" wheezed the driver, as Sam clung round his neck. "I'm only doing my job."

"Me and Jenkins haven't got any money," wailed the gunman. "The folk in the coach have plenty though."

"Lily-livered poltroons!" muttered Ned, pushing their captives off the coach and swinging to the ground after them. Sam and Fernando jumped down beside him.

A tangle of arms and legs and shells on sticks appeared at the window of the coach. The occupants were squealing and yelping as they were dragged one by one onto the road.

"This is an outrage!" screamed a ruddy-faced man in a fine silver and white coat. He was shaking so hard with anger that his huge curly wig looked ready to topple.

His gaze swept over the pirates and Sam noticed Charlie shrink back out of sight.

"Don't you know who my father is?" demanded a snooty young boy, dressed in a bright green silk jacket and breeches.

"Indeed I do," said Captain Blade. He waved the rifle that had been knocked from the gunman's hand. "He is Mr Oliver Castle and he is going to lend us his coach and his money – and all these fine clothes!"

As he spoke the pirates moved forward menacingly.

"You villain!" yelped Mr Castle, holding a terrified servant boy in front of him like a shield. "Who do you think you are?"

Captain Blade thought for a moment. "Mr Black at your service," he said smoothly.

"But there's been some mistake," blustered Castle. "I was coming to meet you at the tavern!"

"I changed my mind," said Blade. "I've decided to take the money and keep the ship. And I'll let you into a little secret. The name's really Blackheart, Captain Blackheart of the *Grinning Skull.*" There was a gasp of shock from the captives. "I see you've heard of me."

Brilliant! thought Sam. *We get our ship back and Castle will think it was Blackheart that tricked him!*

"Now, time's pressing," the captain went on, "so if you'll just remove your clothes we'll disguise ourselves as you and be on our way."

He stared for a moment at Oliver Castle's clean-shaven face. "Ben," he called.

"You're the right size for Mr Castle's clothes but you'll have to lose the beard."

"But Captain!" protested Ben in horror.

"I'll shave him," said Peter.

Fernando tossed Peter the gunman's knife and he dragged Ben off to the stream.

"You, boy," said the captain, putting a hand on Charlie's shoulder and making sure that Castle didn't get a look at her face. "You can play the son. You're about the right height although you're not a simpering ninny like him! Fernando, Peter, you can squeeze into the servants' clothes." He handed the rifle to Ned. "I'll be Jenkins the driver and you can sit with me."

With some rude oaths from Ben as his beard was scraped away, the pirates were soon ready in their disguises.

"Outrageous!" spluttered Oliver Castle

when he and his people had been trussed
up and marched into the forest. "I'll have
you hanged for this!"

Captain Blade, now dressed in the
driver's oversized coat and floppy hat,
made him a sweeping bow. "You'll have
to catch us first," he said pleasantly. "And
I doubt you'll be chasing after us in your
undergarments."

As they got to the coach Ben opened the
door for Charlie. "Come on, Augustus,
my son. You look good in your finery.

You'll have to teach me to talk posh before we get to the town." He wriggled uncomfortably in Castle's fancy shoes and rubbed his newly shaven face. "I wouldn't have agreed to this if I'd known I'd have to lose my beard," he complained. "You could have gone kinder with the knife, Peter."

Peter clambered into the coach with him. "Only doing my duty as your serving man, sir," he said, buttoning up his borrowed livery.

Blade and Ned climbed up onto the driver's seat, pulling their borrowed hats low over their faces.

"Our own mothers wouldn't recognise us," laughed Ned.

Meanwhile, Fernando, in the young servant's uniform, was hauling two heavy money bags out of the coach. Each was half full of gold coins.

"What are you doing?" asked Sam.

"That's Castle's payment for the ship. We can't buy her back without it."

"Blackheart will get his due," said Fernando, with a wink. He tipped all the coins into one bag, filled the other with stones, hefted them back into the coach and climbed aboard.

Sam climbed in behind him, Crow clamped to his shoulder. He wondered if Fernando had barnacles in his brain. "You can't offer Blackheart a bag of pebbles!" he hissed in his ear. "He'll never fall for it. He'll realise we've tricked him."

But Fernando just grinned. "Wait and see," he said mysteriously.

CHAPTER ELEVEN

As the coach clattered into the main square, Sam could see the townsfolk glancing over with looks of fear and loathing.

"I don't think Mr Castle's very popular," he said.

"He isn't," said Charlie. "If we get away with this we'll be doing most people a favour."

"Don't let your faces be seen," warned Ben. "We don't want anyone knowing it's not him till the deed's done."

Captain Blade brought the coach to a halt. A narrow alley led down to the sea.

"Take that road, lad," Ned told Sam. "You'll get to the jetty much quicker — and without being seen with us."

"Yo ho ho!" squawked Crow in his ear, as the coach sped away.

"You need to keep out of sight," said Sam, coaxing the parrot onto his finger. "Blackheart might remember that you attacked him if he sees you with me." He held his hand up and Crow flew after the coach with a loud screech.

Sam sprinted down the cobbled path to the jetty. He could see the *Sea Wolf* straight ahead. He felt as if there were jellyfish in his tummy. He'd been gone a long time. What was Blackheart going to say?

The villain was standing on the deck

with his henchmen around him. He was practising a false smile, ready to meet Oliver Castle. Taking a deep breath, Sam ran up the gangplank. Blackheart saw him

and his face turned red with anger.

"Where have you been, you laggardy lumpfish?" he demanded, giving him a shove.

"I'm sorry, Captain," yelped Sam as he stumbled across the deck. "But my mother hadn't seen me for an age and she gave me lots of jobs to do." He bent his head and wrung his hands. "She's a poor widow with no one in the world to care for her . . ."

He broke off and slipped the crew a quick glance. They were all murmuring about their mothers. One was even wiping away a tear. But Hooknose was standing slightly apart, staring hard at him.

"And when I went to leave she got very upset because she'd seen a man following me and she thought he was after me," Sam went on quickly. "I had to wait until she stopped crying." Hooknose shifted uneasily and suddenly became very busy winding up a coil of rope.

"Humph! Well, you'll just have to make up for lost time!" snapped Blackheart, turning away to stand at the port rail. "Get swabbing!"

Sam heard the rattle of the carriage and the horses' hooves clattering on the cobbled jetty as he bent to his work. His palms felt sticky with sweat. If this went wrong, they'd all be in deadly danger. One of Blackheart's men crouched beside him and nudged his elbow.

"See the gentry!" he cackled, displaying a mouth full of rotten teeth.

Ben and Charlie got down from the coach. Watching them strutting up the gangplank, Sam had to hide a grin. Charlie was holding a lacy handkerchief to her nose as if she couldn't stand the smell. It was a clever move as it hid her features. Captain Blade and Ned stayed on the driver's seat with their hats pulled down over their faces. Fernando and Peter stood by the coach door like dutiful servants.

Sam noticed Fernando had wrapped a cloak around himself despite the warmth of the afternoon.

"Which of you is Mr Black?" asked Ben, looking down his nose at the crew. Sam wanted to laugh but he knew he couldn't. Ben was talking in a funny strangled voice as he tried to be posh.

"That would be me," said Blackheart stepping forward. "Mr Castle? And you've brought the gold?"

"'old your 'orses, my good sir!" exclaimed Ben. "We'll need to hinspect the boat first!"

Sam saw Blackheart frown at this but he stepped aside and motioned for his visitors to go where they pleased. He stared long and hard at Charlie.

Has he recognised her? Sam wondered, his heart thudding.

"Is this your son?" Blackheart asked at last.

"Yes, this is Augustus," answered Ben. "I'm buying the vessil for 'im."

"A fine ship for a fine strapping lad," growled Blackheart. Sam saw him mutter something to one of his crew and caught the words, "he's so small he's more like a sprat!" His crewmen smirked at this.

Blackheart led the way to the poop deck, his henchmen scampering quickly out of the way. Sam noticed they had fresh scratches on their arms and hands. He knew who'd done that. Sinbad must be alive – and on board still. And as if Sam had called him, the black cat appeared,

hissing, in the doorway of the galley. This was a disaster. If Sinbad saw his beloved Charlie he'd run over to her and give the game away!

CHAPTER TWELVE

A pirate with his arm in a dirty sling
ducked behind Sam at the sight of
the mangy moggy.

"That fiend from hell attacks without
warning," he growled. "He's had me twice,
so I reckon it's your turn."

"We'll soon see about that!" said Sam.
He sped over and slammed the galley door
in the cat's face. They heard Sinbad yowl

and scratch at the wood. "Castle will get a shock when that monster's let loose!" he said with a chuckle.

"I'd love to see that," sniggered the pirate with the sling. "But by then we'll be long gone on the *Grinning Skull* and counting our gold!"

Ben and Charlie were coming back down to the main deck with Blackheart. "Where did you get this boat?" Ben was asking.

Blackheart gave a cunning smile. "I got her from someone who can't sail any more. Let's say he's . . . indisposed."

Sam saw a brief look of anger pass over Ben's face. "I've seen better vessils," he said at last. "But the boy wants 'er so I suppose she'll do."

Blackheart rubbed his hands together. "At the agreed price?"

Ben nodded. "At the agreed price."

Sam could see the delight in Blackheart's eyes at the thought that he'd finally had the last laugh over Captain Blade, his despised enemy.

"The gold's in my coach," Ben announced, making for the gangplank.

"Pieces of eight!" came a loud squawk. Crow had appeared on the top of the mainmast.

To Sam's horror, Blackheart pulled his gun from his belt and aimed it at the bird.

"You won't have to put up with that vermin," he growled.

"No!" cried Charlie. Everyone spun round to stare at her. "I want the parrot. Father, make him give me the parrot."

"Very well," said Ben. "Leave the bird, Mr Black." Sam nearly sank to the deck in relief.

"Saves me a bullet," grunted Blackheart, striding towards the gangplank. "Let's see the colour of your money and we're done."

Keeping up his job of swabbing the decks, Sam watched them go down to the coach. He hoped Fernando hadn't switched the bags now that Blackheart had demanded to see the gold. They couldn't risk anything going wrong when the *Sea Wolf* was nearly theirs again.

Ben handed the heavy bag to Blackheart, who opened it straightaway. Sam held his breath as the evil pirate plunged his arm inside and pulled out a handful of . . .

gold coins. He ordered one of his men to count it out.

"It's all there, Captain," came the report at last.

The man stood guard over the bag, arms folded and looking important. Ben thrust out his hand to Blackheart. Sam was glad to see that he was still wearing Oliver Castle's gloves. One look at his rough and calloused skin and their enemy would have smelled a rat for sure.

"Deal!" cried Blackheart, shaking hands.

"Hexcellent," said Ben in his posh voice. He turned to Blade and Ned who still sat on the coach with their heads turned away. "Jenkins and . . . er . . . Nedkins . . . I 'ave a fancy to take the boat out right away. Get on board and put some sails up on them pole things." He snapped his fingers at Fernando and Peter. "You two 'elp 'em."

Fernando, still wrapped in the cloak, looked half asleep. He jerked into life, stumbled against the pirate guarding the gold and went sprawling on the ground.

"My apologies," he muttered, getting to his feet and straightening the man's jacket. Then he scampered on board after Blade. Ben and Charlie swept along behind him.

Charlie strutted round the deck. "Keep yourself out of sight, Sam," she muttered as she passed. "With luck the blaggard won't notice you're still on board until we're under sail."

Sam ducked down beside the wheel.

Peter and Ned were pulling feebly on one of the ropes, pretending they'd never hoisted a sail in their lives. The mainsail inched slowly into place. Sam longed for the ship to be out on the high seas — and safe from Blackheart. He hardly

dared breathe as he felt the wind start
to catch the sail. They'd be off any minute.

"Sam! Where is that dratted boy?"
The dreaded voice boomed up to the
deck. Blackheart strode onto the
gangplank.

Sam looked desperately at his friends.
There was no way they could protect him
without weapons. He'd have to leave the
ship. He stood up.

"I'm here," he said faintly.

"Move your lazy bones and get ashore!"

"I won't have it, Father!" yelled Charlie,
stamping her foot. "This ship is filthy and
they're taking that servant boy away before
he's finished cleaning."

"The lad can come on our little trip,"
Ben called to Blackheart. "He could do 'is
work while we sail."

Sam's hopes rose.

"No," sneered Blackheart. "We've shaken
on the deal. You take the ship as she is.

Get down here now, Sam, if you don't want to be skinned alive."

Sam had no choice. He walked forlornly to the jetty, ducking a swipe from Blackheart as he passed. Now his friends had all the sails up.

"Mr Black," called Ben from the deck. "Would one of your fine men be so good as to undo that rope what is keeping us tied 'ere."

"They'll never get her moving!" Hooknose scoffed as he tossed the *Sea Wolf's* mooring rope over her rail.

Blackheart beamed at his crewmates. "And if they do they'll likely sink her before they get out of the harbour," he guffawed. "I only wish Blade were still alive to see his precious ship in the hands of such landlubbers."

Trying not to show how desperate he felt, Sam stood watching as Ned and Fernando heaved up the gangplank and the ship

began to move away from the jetty. His
crew had won the *Sea Wolf* back, but
they'd had to leave him behind – with
Blackheart.

Chapter Thirteen

Sam watched helplessly as the *Sea Wolf* moved away from her mooring towards the open sea. A terrible thought leapt into his brain. Maybe his magic coin didn't have the power to take him back to the future when he wasn't on his own ship! If it didn't, he'd be stuck here forever, part of Blackheart's evil crew!

"Let's feast our eyes on our gold,

mateys!" declared the jubilant pirate
captain, tipping the bag upside-down.

There was a dull clatter as a pile of
pebbles fell onto the cobbles. Blackheart's
mouth dropped open.

"The rat-faced varmints!" he bellowed.
"We've been tricked."

Sam made sure he looked as gobsmacked
as the rest of the crew, but inside he
wanted to cheer. Fernando must have
switched the bags when he'd bumped
into Blackheart's man. His crew had the
gold *and* their ship. If only he was with
them!

"Sam, look lively!" came a cry from the
Sea Wolf. The ship had reached the end
of the jetty! Captain Blade had taken off
his disguise and was standing in full view
of Blackheart at the stern rail. Fernando
stood at his side, swinging a rope round
his head.

Sam didn't waste a second. He sprinted

down the jetty as if he was going for an
Olympic gold medal.

He heard an angry roar behind him.
"It's Blade and his men, curses upon them!
They've double-crossed us! Get that boy."

Heavy footsteps pounded after Sam.
Hooknose was leading the pack.

Sam reached the end of the jetty.

"Got yer!" bellowed Hooknose, making
a dive for him.

"Jump!" yelled Fernando.

Sam leapt off the end of the jetty just as Fernando's rope came snaking down from the ship. Sam grabbed it and swung through the air, bracing himself as his feet hit the hull.

"We've got you!" cried Charlie. She and Fernando pulled the rope up as fast as they could.

WHZZZZ! A sound like a jet-propelled

bee zipped past Sam's ear and splinters of wood went flying from the hull. Blackheart was firing at him! He swung from side to side to avoid the shots. At last he reached the rail and Fernando and Charlie hauled him to safety.

"Get down!" warned the captain.

They all flung themselves flat on the deck as another bullet screamed past.

"Thanks for rescuing me," gulped Sam breathlessly.

"It must be time for one of your high fives," said Fernando.

"Low five, you mean," laughed Sam. "I don't want my fingers shot off."

Lying on the deck, they slapped palms.

Sam peeped through the rail for a quick look back at the jetty. Blackheart stood there, smoking pistols in his hands.

"You swindling swamp slug!" he screamed.

"Swamp slug!" squawked Crow from the top of the mast.

The *Sea Wolf* moved slowly past the headland and into open sea, the small crew struggling to unfurl more sails. Puerto Caballo was lost from sight.

"Now back to the island to rescue our friends," declared Captain Blade. "Sam, get your keen Silver eyes on lookout."

Sam had his foot on the rigging ready to climb up to the crow's nest, when something caught his eye. A galleon was coming into view round the headland behind them. Even from here he could see the dark sails and red skull and crossbones flying from her mast. "Ship ahoy, off Columbus Point!" he cried. "It's the *Grinning Skull.*"

"We can't outrun them with only seven men," cried the captain. "Get ready for battle!"

"But we've got no cannonballs or powder!" shouted Ben. "Blackheart cleaned us out."

"No he didn't," said Sam quickly. "I hid some." He led them down to the gun deck.

"Well, bowl me to Bridgetown in a barrel!" gasped Ned when he saw the hidden ammunition under the floorboards. "We stand a fighting chance after all."

"Excellent work, Sam," said the captain. "Mr Black's going to get quite a surprise when we fire first!"

"And we've got this!" said Sam, proudly producing the *Sea Wolf* flag.

Everyone cheered and slapped him on the back.

"Get that up and flying, Ben," ordered Blade. "I'll be at the wheel. Sam and Fernando stand by the sails. The rest of you charge the guns. The moment we go broadsides — we fire."

As the *Sea Wolf* turned her starboard side towards Blackheart's ship, her cannon roared, sending a thunderous rumble through the deck. One of the shots tore a hole in the enemy's mainsail.

"I wish I could see their faces," laughed Ben. "They thought we were defenceless."

The *Grinning Skull* returned fire. Sam felt the ship rock with the force of the barrage as the cannonballs hit the water dangerously close to the hull.

Blade brought the *Sea Wolf* round for another pass.

"Bullseye!" yelled Sam as he saw huge splinters of wood exploding into the air. "That landed right on their foredeck."

Charlie ran up, her face grave. "We've only got one cannonball left, Captain."

"Then we'll make it count," Blade bellowed. "Haul on those sheets, boys, we're coming about."

Now Blackheart's ship was so close Sam could see the gunners at the starboard cannon. He gulped. There was no way the enemy could miss from this range. But the cannonballs didn't come. And now Sam saw why.

Another vessel was heading in from the open sea and making straight for the *Grinning Skull*. Blackheart was screaming at his men. "We're being attacked on both sides! Charge the port cannon or I'll slit yer throats."

"Fire!" shouted Blade. The last cannonball smashed into the enemy's hull,

leaving a gaping hole. At once Blackheart's ship tilted violently as it began to take on water. Pirates were jumping overboard in panic.

"Victory!" cried Fernando. "The rats are leaving the sinking ship."

Charlie ran to the rail and peered out at the other vessel. "She's changed course," she gasped. "She's coming for us and we've got no ammunition left."

Sam studied the approaching ship.

"She couldn't attack a pilchard!" he exclaimed. "Her sails are all tattered and the mainmast's shored up with planks. The hull looks ready to spring a leak at any moment." His eyes fell on the painted name. "It's the *Lady Eliza* from the island!" he gasped.

Now everyone could see Harry Hopp at the wheel and the rest of their crewmates waving from the rail.

"By Poseidon!" chuckled Captain Blade. "They mended the old tub and sailed all the way here!"

The *Sea Wolf* sped away from Hispaniola, under full sail. Harry Hopp and his men had come aboard, leaving the Lady Eliza to float where she would.

"You did a good job there," said Ned, casting an expert eye back at the abandoned vessel.

"We had a few scary moments on our voyage," Harry told him. "But none so scary as seeing Ben Hudson without a beard!"

"I'll thank you to speak respectful-like to me," said Ben, brushing imaginary dust off the fine coat he was still wearing. "I'm gentry, I am."

"Seems we've got lots of stories to tell each other," chuckled Harry, as he made Ben a deep bow.

Everyone laughed except for Charlie.

"What's the matter?" asked Sam.

"I can't find Sinbad," she said anxiously. "Something must have happened to him."

"I know where he is!" exclaimed Sam. He ran to the galley door and flung it open. "Look out, everyone."

Yowling angrily, Sinbad launched himself onto the deck. The pirates backed off as he flashed his claws at them.

"Sinbad!" cried Charlie. The cat stopped dead, then threw himself onto his back at her feet, purring loudly. Charlie bent down and rubbed his tummy lovingly.

"To Tortuga!" declared the captain, holding up the bag of gold. "We'll have a feast there with Mr Black's money."

"Pieces of meat!" squawked Crow from Sam's shoulder.

"And we'll get some nice seed for the bird," said Blade, edging away.

"I could always cook something," suggested Peter. "There might be a few scraps left in the galley."

"NO!" yelled the crew.

"I'll eat nothin' but the best food!" announced Ben, adjusting his silk cravat, "now that I'm an 'igh born gent."

"You'll not get that from Peter," laughed Ned, slapping the cook on the back.

"Won't Blackheart be on our tail as

· 138 ·

soon as he's repaired his vessel?" asked
Harry.

"He'll have other things on his mind,"
Blade told him. "Mr Castle will be setting
the authorities on him. I think I may
have given him the impression that it was
Blackheart who stole his money and his
coach."

"And left him in his underwear!"
chuckled Fernando.

"This has been an awesome adventure,"
Sam said to Charlie. "And I'm—"

He broke off suddenly.

"What's the matter?" asked Charlie.

"My fingers and toes are tingling,"
whispered Sam. "I'm off home."

"Hide," hissed Charlie. "You can't let
anyone see you disappear."

Sam leapt behind a barrel. The bright
Caribbean faded away as he was caught up
in a whirlwind. The next instant he found
himself sprawled on his bedroom floor on

top of his school project.

Sam sat up and stared at it. He knew exactly what he was going to put on his family shield now. A fierce battle showing the victorious *Sea Wolf*, and the *Grinning Skull* sinking below the waves. He couldn't wait to tell his whole class how it happened.

But then he remembered. He couldn't tell anyone. His pirate adventures had to remain hush-hush.

Maybe it would have to be the haddock and chips on the shield after all. But, no! His teacher had said it had to show something interesting about his family. He was descended from a pirate so a pirate battle was the perfect image for his shield.

No one needed to know that he'd actually been there at the time. That was all part of being an undercover pirate – you never gave away your secrets!

CREW MANIFEST

Sinbad

Crow

Thomas Blade
Captain

Peter Craddock
Ship's Cook

Fernando
Rigger

Don't miss the next exciting adventure in the
Sam Silver: Undercover Pirate series

THE GREAT RESCUE

Available in June 2013!
Read on for a special preview
of the first chapter.

CHAPTER ONE

Sam Silver stood at his back door, frowning at the stilts in his hands. Why was it so hard to balance on them? The woman at the Circus Skills class had run around the school hall on hers and they'd been really long.

There was only a small concrete yard behind his parents' fish and chip shop, and with no garden it didn't give him much space to practise. But that wasn't going to stop Sam. So far he'd managed three and a half seconds before he'd toppled onto the bins. The noise had brought his father running, a piece of battered cod in his hand. At least Sam had given his dad a good laugh. But he wanted applause. He wanted to be the best stilt-walker in Backwater Bay. Actually he'd be the *only* stilt-walker in Backwater Bay as the Circus Skills woman had only handed out one pair, but that didn't matter.

He stood on an old oil can and grasped the stilts again. He hoisted himself onto them and swayed, leaning against the drainpipe for balance. Then he stepped forward. This time it felt different. He was still upright for a start. He took another step and another, feeling more confident with each one.

"Awesome!" he cried as he staggered

towards the fence. "Eight steps. That must
be a world record!"

He swung his leg round to make a turn
and at once he realised his mistake. He was
spinning too fast. He crashed down on a
pile of cardboard boxes, squashing them
flat. But he wasn't going to give up now.
Using the washing line, he hauled himself
up and set off for the back door, avoiding
his mother's pot plants. This time he made
it and leapt down onto the steps in triumph.

"Success!" he yelled up at the seagulls swirling over the bay.

He couldn't wait to show his friend Fernando. Fernando might be an expert juggler but he couldn't walk on stilts. Sam wanted to demonstrate straight away. There was only one problem with this. Fernando lived on a pirate ship in the Caribbean — three hundred years ago. Well, that *would* have been a problem for anyone else, but not for Sam. Sam had a magic doubloon, a gold coin sent to him by an old pirate ancestor, Joseph Silver. He could go back in time whenever he wanted and have an adventure with Captain Blade, Fernando and the bold crew of the *Sea Wolf*. He wouldn't be able to take his stilts as only his clothes time-travelled with him, but there was always spare wood on the ship and he was sure he'd be able to make some.

Sam sprinted up to his bedroom and changed into the old T-shirt and jeans he

always wore for his pirate adventures. He
didn't have to worry about his parents
wondering where he'd gone.
The coin would bring him
back to exactly the same
time in the present as
when he left.

He grabbed the
ancient bottle that
stood on his shelf.
Tipping out the gold
doubloon, he spat on it
and gave it a rub. At once, his bedroom
walls began to spin around him and he was
sucked up into the familiar whirling tunnel
that always made him feel he was inside
a giant vacuum cleaner. Then everything
stopped turning and he landed with a
bump on the hard wooden floor of the *Sea
Wolf*'s storeroom.

The ship was gently swaying. Sam
jumped up and ran over to a barrel where a

jerkin, belt, neckerchief and spyglass were lying. His friend Charlie always made sure they were ready for him when he returned to the past. She was the only one who knew he was from the twenty-first century and even she found it hard to believe. He quickly dressed in his pirate outfit, tucked his spyglass into his belt and left the storeroom ready for action.

The hot midday sun beat down on his head as he bounded up the steps to the main deck. A hearty sea shanty filled the air and when he got to the top of the stairs he saw the crew busy mending sails and splicing rope. Beyond the rail he could see that the ship was at anchor in a quiet bay.

"Sam Silver!" came a surprised shout and Harry Hopp, the first mate, dropped his rope and came stomping over to him, his wooden leg pounding on the deck. He patted him hard on the back, sending Sam staggering. "Shiver me timbers, we're more than a thousand miles away from where we saw you last," he declared, his grizzled face beaming. "How did you get here so quick?"

Sam gulped. When the coin took him back to his own time his shipmates thought he'd just gone off to see his poor widowed mother and help her on her farm. But that wasn't going to explain how he'd managed to whiz across the ocean to be with them when he'd finished milking the cow and mucking out the pig. Speedboats hadn't been invented in 1706!

"He's a true Silver," called Ned the bosun. "Nothing keeps him from his crew."

"Aye!" chorused his shipmates.

Phew! thought Sam. It was useful being descended from a famous pirate. Joseph Silver had been well loved by the pirates and his family could do no wrong.

"By Neptune's trident, we're glad to see you," came a deep voice. A tall man with belts full of weapons and red braids in his beard was striding across the deck to greet him. It was Captain Blade. "With an extra pair of hands we'll have these sails stitched and seaworthy in no time."

Someone gave him a friendly shove from behind. Sam whipped round to find Fernando grinning at him.

"Greetings, my friend," he said, his Spanish accent strong in his excitement at seeing Sam. "Perhaps you could swab the decks instead. Last time you were let loose with a needle you stitched your jerkin to your breeches."

"My sewing's not that bad!" protested Sam. "But wait. I've got something amazing to show you before I start my duties. I'll just find some wood and then . . ."

"Pieces of eight!" A bright green parrot landed on Sam's head and peered down into his face. "Ahoy, me hearty!" he squawked.

"Hello, Crow," said Sam, coaxing the parrot onto his finger.

He saw the captain give the bird a nervous glance so he took Crow away to the side rail. Captain Blade feared no man but he was terrified of parrots. Fernando said it was because a parrot had stolen his favourite teething ring when he was a baby but all the pirates had a different story to tell. Sam was only allowed to keep his feathered friend if everyone pretended he was in fact just a rather brightly-coloured crow.

"So what's this amazing new thing, Sam?" asked Fernando.

"You'll love it," began Sam. "I've learnt how to——"

"Sam!" Charlie came running up, pushing her bandana back off her forehead. "I'm glad you're here. Wait till you see what Sinbad can do!" Charlie had a mangy black cat draped round her shoulders. Sam and Fernando backed off as he gave them a baleful glare. Sinbad was a loyal crew member but he was quick with his claws if anyone but Charlie tried to touch him.

"I was just about to show—" protested Sam.

"Sinbad's so clever," crooned Charlie, ignoring him. "I've taught him to sing for his supper!" She produced a smelly fish head from her pocket and dangle it in front of the cat's nose. In a flash Sinbad jumped down on the deck, sat bolt upright and set up an ear-piercing wail. Everyone blocked their ears in horror until Charlie threw the fish head down and he devoured it in two gulps.

"What do you think?" said Charlie in delight.

"Very good," answered Sam shakily. "Or it would be if he could keep the volume down." He brightened up. "Time for my trick at last. You'll be so impressed—"

TWA-ANG! There was a strange whistling sound and an arrow thudded into the mast, narrowly missing the captain's head.

"We're under attack!" cried Fernando.

the orion star

Sign up for **the orion star** newsletter to get inside information about your favourite children's authors as well as exclusive competitions and early reading copy giveaways.

www.orionbooks.co.uk/newsletters